RICKY VARGAS:

Born to Be Funny!

To Andrew, David, and Nathan . . .
three boys who make me laugh and make me proud.
—A. K.

To mi amigos, Ricky and Mike ... thanks for the laughs!
With special thanks to Matt.
—S. C.

No part of this publication may be reproduced, stored in a retrieval system, or transmitted in any
form or by any means, electronic, mechanical, photocopying, recording, or otherwise, without writ-
ten permission of the publisher. For information regarding permission, write to Scholastic Inc.,
Attention: Permissions Department, 557 Broadway, New York, NY 10012.

Text copyright © 2011 by Alan Katz.
Illustrations copyright © 2011 by Scholastic Inc.

Illustrations by Stacy Curtis.
All rights reserved. Published by Scholastic Inc.
SCHOLASTIC, LITTLE APPLE, and associated logos are trademarks and/or
registered trademarks of Scholastic Inc.

Library of Congress Cataloging-in-Publication Data is available.

ISBN 978-0-545-24584-5

10 9 8 7 6 5 4 3 2 1   11 12 13 14 15

Printed in the U.S.A. 40
First school market edition, February 2011

RICKY VARGAS:

Born to Be Funny!

by Alan Katz

with illustrations by Stacy Curtis

LITTLE APPLE

Scholastic Inc.

New York   Toronto   London   Auckland   Sydney   Mexico City   New Delhi   Hong Kong

Check out
other books about Ricky!

Ricky Vargas: The Funniest Kid in the World

Table of Contents

The Vargish Story 1

The Unfunny Day Story 24

Extra: How to Be the Funniest Kid in the World 50

The Vargish Story

Gax ree!

"I can't believe we have French homework," Eddie moaned as he and Ricky walked home from school.

"Listen, we're lucky," said Ricky. "In Paris, kids have to do all of their homework in French!"

"Math is in French, science is in French…"

"I get it!" said Eddie.
"…they even have to take Spanish lessons in French!" added Ricky.

"That's ridiculous," said Eddie.

"Hey, it's not my idea," Ricky
told him.

Ricky and Eddie were best friends
and next-door neighbors.

Except when they were mad at
each other.

In that case, they weren't best
friends for a little while, but
they were still next-door neighbors
(because it was too hard to move
every time they had a fight).

Eddie liked laughing along with Ricky. But he didn't know what to do when Ricky said...

That night, Ricky worked and
worked and worked and worked,
and after five minutes, he had
come up with a whole new way
of speaking.

It wasn't English.

It wasn't French.

It wasn't anything anyone had
ever heard before.

It was...

VARGISH!

"Good morning, Ricky," said
Mrs. Wilder.

Mrs. Wilder knew something
was up, because that was a
strange answer, even for Ricky.

"He is speaking Vargish,"
Eddie said to the teacher.
"It's his new language."

"Ricky, greb num pla pla
delp!" Mrs. Wilder said.

She was trying to say, "Please
stop talking that way."

But she didn't really know Vargish.

To Ricky, that meant "Please
put a book on your head
and hop up and down 27 times."

And so he did.

Before long, Vargish became very popular.

15

Even the teachers were speaking it.

Vargish was taking over the whole school!

And guess what happened next....

Kaba blee blee demby voo!

Oops!

What happened was
Ricky stood up and shouted...

19

And just like that, the teachers and students all went back to speaking English.

And everything was exactly as
it had been before.

Well, almost everything...

"I can't believe we have Vargish homework," Eddie moaned as he and Ricky walked home from school.

The Unfunny Day Story

Everyone who has ever met
Ricky Vargas says he's the
funniest kid in the world.

His mom says so. His dad says so.
So does his violin teacher, his
mailman, his baseball coach,
and his aunt Jen.

Now, of course, those people haven't met *all the other* kids in the world, so there *may* be a funnier kid somewhere. But if so, they haven't met him. Or her.

Ricky does funny things.
Ricky says funny things.
And just by being himself,
he's made people's lives happier
for all 2,704 days
he's been alive.

Until today.

See, when Ricky woke up this morning, Ricky felt *funny*... because he didn't feel funny.

He got dressed in very serious
clothes.

He ate a very serious breakfast.

And he had a very serious chat
with his parents.

Ricky's mom felt his head.

Ricky's dad looked in his throat.

But it was clear Ricky wasn't sick—
he just wasn't funny.

And in the classroom,
when Mrs. Wilder asked,

Ricky didn't say, "All of them," to make everyone laugh.

Ricky wasn't funny
at recess. Or at lunch.
Or anywhere.

His buddy Eddie did his
best to help.

And it made everyone say...

It was weird, but when the funniest kid stopped being funny, everyone else stopped laughing.

Good thing Eddie came up
with a plan.

He said, "Maybe if we make
Ricky laugh, he'll start making
us laugh again!"

The rest of the day, everyone
tried to make Ricky laugh.

His teacher tried.

His friends tried.

Even his principal tried.

43

Just before the end of this
very serious day, it was
time for science.

Mrs. Wilder showed the
class how sliced onion
makes most people cry.

She sliced...and everyone cried.

Everyone *except* Ricky.

He just laughed. And laughed.
And laughed and laughed
and laughed. He giggled.
And even snorted once or twice.

And even though they were crying, Ricky's teacher and friends were happy, because they could tell that tomorrow...

...Ricky Vargas would be the funniest kid in the world once again!

49

How to Be the Funniest Kid in the World

What Would Ricky Do?

Ricky Vargas is the funniest kid in the world. Maybe that's why he sometimes does things a little differently than you or I might. To see for yourself, rearrange the letters in bold to form a word that would make sense in each sentence.

1. What will Ricky be when he grows up? Who knows, he could be America's funniest **DINER PEST**!

_ _ _ _ _ _ _ _ _ _

2. Ricky likes to run in the park and wave to the **PIG NOSE**.

_ _ _ _ _ _ _ _

3. Looking for Ricky? You can be sure he's out on the field playing **SEAL BLAB**.

_ _ _ _ _ _ _ _ _

4. Ricky watches the weather report, and if it's going to rain, he always brings his **LAMB RULE**.

_ _ _ _ _ _ _ _ _

Answers on page 58

Ricky, if I have 20 nickels in my left pocket, and 25 dimes in my right pocket, what does that make?

A lot of noise!

Ricky, this cotton candy doesn't taste right!

That's odd, I made it with real cotton!

53

Vargish-English Dictionary

Vargish
"Frek naga jik jik?"
"Leppy vabo!"
"Croof wiv bloberoo?"
"Quabba."
"Gax ree!"

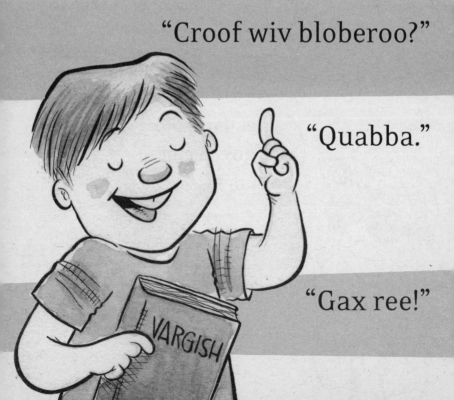

English

"Would you like to smell my pickle breath?"

"There's a baby camel in my backpack!"

"Mrs. Wilder, will you be teaching this class in 3-D?"

"I'll meet you in the library at 12:29, and we can work on the science project and make a poster about U.S. states that start with the letter *M*."

"Today's school lunch is hot fudge salami."

The World's a Funny Place

On Ricky's unfunny day, who was the funniest kid in the world? You decide!

PIERRE DE LA VARGAS, FRANCE

SKIPPY VARGAS, AUSTRALIA

SIR RICHARD VARGAS, UK

Any of them might have been the funniest. Or perhaps it was YOU!

Answers (from page 51):

1. PRESIDENT
2. PIGEONS
3. BASEBALL
4. UMBRELLA